W9-AZQ-135

"I have many names," the Indian said. "White men call me Crazy Panther. I am called shaman by my people. Crooked Foot Billie is the name given to me by my father."

"Crooked Foot Billie," Walter mumbled to himself. Where had he heard that name before?

Crooked Foot sat in front of the campfire and removed a sharp knife from a sheath on his belt. He tested the blade with his thumb and smiled at Walter.

Suddenly, horror engulfed Walter as he remembered where he'd heard the Indian's name before. He started to tremble.

Crooked Foot was the ghost the bus driver had told him about!

Read all the Tales from the Crypt:

A TALE FROM CAMP CRYPT

A TALE FROM THE CRYPT CARNIVAL

NAME YOUR NIGHTMARE
A Find Your (Unfortunate) Fate™ Book

TALES FROM THE CRYPT
Volumes 1–5

JOKES FROM THE CRYPT

A TALE FROM CAMP CRYPT

by Vincent Courtney

Bullseye Books
Random House 🏠 New York

A BULLSEYE BOOK PUBLISHED BY RANDOM HOUSE, INC.
Copyright © 1995 by William M. Gaines, Agent, Inc. All rights
reserved under International and Pan-American Copyright
Conventions. Published in the United States by Random House, Inc.,
New York, and simultaneously in Canada by Random House of
Canada Limited, Toronto.

Library of Congress Catalog Card Number: 94-69505
ISBN: 0-679-87474-7
RL: 5.3

Manufactured in the United States of America
10 9 8 7 6 5 4 3 2 1

1
MOTHER KNOWS WORST

"Why, Walter Ridgemont the third! What an absolutely horrible thing to ask your mother!"

Mrs. Eudora Ridgemont's hands fluttered to her chest as she tried to keep from fainting. She and her eleven-year-old son sat in the living room of the Ridgemont summer estate.

At that moment, Buffy Ridgemont, Walter's sister, came in. She wore a summer dress that cost more than most people's entire wardrobes. She sipped lemonade from a priceless crystal glass.

"Mother dear, whatever could be the matter?" she asked.

Mrs. Ridgemont wrinkled her nose as if smelling a leaky sewer pipe. "Walter just asked me if he could go to…" She began fanning herself as another fainting spell came on. "If he could go to…*ahem*…summer camp!"

The ten-year-old girl choked on her drink. "Summer camp? How perfectly awful!"

Mrs. Ridgemont took a deep breath, then turned to her son. "Buffy's right, darling," she said. "I mean, really, Walter. Who ever heard of a Ridgemont going to summer camp?"

"But, Momsy!" Walter whined, stamping his $300 ostrich-hide tennis shoes. "I'm so bored!"

"But summer camp is so…so common!" Mrs. Ridgemont replied with a shudder. "All those filthy, brutish children sleeping together in cabins. Ugh!"

"I don't mind," Walter said. He grinned wickedly. *The more peasants to rule over,* he thought.

"But you're so delicate, Walter, and the woods are full of dirty animals and dangerous plants like poison ivy. And the air is bad. Full of pollen and mosquitoes. No, Walter." She wagged a finger at him. "I won't have you suffering through that."

"But, Momsy, I want to go!" Walter said, stamping his feet again. "And nothing you can say will change my mind."

Walter covered his face with his hands and opened his eyes as wide as he could. Concealed under his ring was a smear of menthol. The menthol burned his eyes like crazy, making them water. When he looked up moments later, tears streamed down his cheeks.

"Now, Wally by Golly," Mrs. Ridgemont said, calling Walter by his pet name. She rushed to put her arm around him. "Don't get upset."

Walter saw a crack in his mother's defenses. He pushed away from her and started shouting, "I want to, I want to, I want to!"

Mrs. Ridgemont pursed her lips. "Be reasonable, Wally by Golly. Mother doesn't think camp is the kind of place for a Ridgemont. She doesn't think you'll like it."

"I know *I* wouldn't," Buffy huffed. She smoothed the ruffles of her summer dress and sipped her drink.

Walter shot his sister a look that would spoil a plate of caviar. *Stupid Buffy,* he thought, *don't you know by now that I always get my way?*

He pretended to wipe away his tears, but was really dabbing more menthol into his eyes. Another gush of tears poured down his cheeks.

Walter turned to his mother and started to whine, "*Please* let me go. I want to go to camp. Please, Momsy. Please. Please. *Please.*"

Mrs. Ridgemont sighed and wiped the tears from his face with her napkin.

"Oh, very well," she said. "If that's what my precious Wally by Golly *really* wants, I will let him go to camp."

Walter sniffled and turned to his sister. "And I want Buffy to come with me, so I know somebody there."

"Mother!" Buffy cried in horror. "I will *not* go to summer camp. I just won't!"

Walter started crying again. "Oh, Momsy," he sniffled, "please make Buffy go. I'll miss her terribly if you don't."

And I do want to punish her for trying to ruin my fun, he added to himself.

"Now, Wally by Golly, your sister doesn't want to go," Mrs. Ridgemont said.

"But she has to," Walter wailed, covering his face with his hands. "I'll miss her too much if we are apart for so long." He snuck a peek at his sister and stuck out his tongue.

"Isn't that nice," Mrs. Ridgemont said, smiling sweetly. "He would miss his sister."

She turned to her daughter. "Buffy, you wouldn't want your brother to miss you, would you?"

"Frankly, Mother, I don't care," Buffy said.

"Please, Momsy, make her go," Walter cried.

"Buffy, I'm afraid I must insist," Mrs. Ridgemont said. "After all, it would be better if someone with refinement went along with Walter."

"But, Mother!" Buffy cried.

"No buts, Buffy. I have decided," Mrs. Ridgemont said, folding her arms. "You and Walter are going to summer camp."

"You always take Walter's side," Buffy whined. "That time he set the neighbor's cat on fire, you said it was an accident."

"It was," Walter said, barely able to conceal his smirk.

Buffy ignored him. "And then there was the time he sucked Mrs. Huston's rare Australian parakeet into the vacuum cleaner. Remember that, Mother?"

"Certainly," she said. "Wally by Golly was just trying to clean the bird. Weren't you, dear?"

Walter's smile was like an angel's. He nodded. "The poor little thing had loose feathers all over it."

"There, you see?" Mrs. Ridgemont said, beaming at her son. "Wally by Golly was just trying to help."

Buffy threw up her hands in disgust.

"Now, you and your brother are going to this Camp Pocahauntus, and I won't hear another word about it," Mrs. Ridgemont said. "After all, how bad could it be?"

2
BUFFY THE CAMPFIRE HATER

The bus to Camp Pocahauntus arrived at the Ridgemont estate early Friday morning. It was an old school bus, adorned with a crudely painted forest scene. Malformed deer grazed on bright green grass. A smear of black paint that was supposed to be a bear scratched its back on a smear of brown paint that was supposed to be a tree.

"Oh, how dreadfully tacky!" Buffy cried when she saw the bus. She turned to her mother and grabbed her hand. "Mother, please! Please don't make me go anywhere in that shabby thing. I would be disgraced if any of my friends saw me."

Walter laughed at his sister's discomfort. "I think the bus looks great."

"Mother!" Buffy pleaded.

Mrs. Ridgemont sniffed in agreement. "That

bus does look rather beneath us. Perhaps it would be better if the chauffeur drove you both to camp."

She turned to the butler. "Smithers," Mrs. Ridgemont said, "would you tell Reynolds to bring the car around?"

Buffy smiled at her brother. For once, she was getting her way.

Or so she thought.

"No!" Walter cried. "I want to go on the bus with the other kids!"

"Fine," Mrs. Ridgemont said. "Buffy will take the car."

"No!" Walter shouted. "I want Buffy to come with me." He crossed his arms and sat on the floor.

"But she doesn't want to take the bus, dear," Mrs. Ridgemont said.

"Then I'm not going," Walter huffed. He took a deep breath and held it until his face turned bright red.

The bus driver beeped the horn.

"Ma'am?" Smithers asked. "Should I have the Rolls brought around or not?"

"No," Mrs. Ridgemont sighed. "I wouldn't want to upset my Wally by Golly. He and his sister will be taking the bus."

The smile dropped off Buffy's face. It was futile to argue with her mother when it came to Walter.

"Time to go," Walter said, grinning at his sister. "Smithers, get the bags."

The aged butler picked up their luggage and carried it out to the bus while the Ridgemonts said their good-byes.

"Give Momsy a kiss," Mrs. Ridgemont said, bending down to her son.

Walter pecked her cheek like a bird sampling poisoned seeds. "Bye," he said as he ran out the front door.

"Good-bye, Buffy dear," Mrs. Ridgemont said, patting her daughter on the head. "Keep an eye on your darling brother."

Buffy faked a smile and trudged out the front door.

Walter turned back and saw his dejected sister walking across the lawn. "Come on, Buffy. We don't want to keep the animals—I mean, the other kids—waiting."

Buffy scowled at him.

Walter laughed and climbed onto the crowded bus.

The bus driver was a withered old man. His sweat-stained baseball cap sat on a greasy mop of stringy hair. He wore a shabby T-shirt that read CAMP POCAHAUNTUS.

"Step right up, kiddies," the driver said in a cracked voice. "I don't bite…unless I get hungry." The old man smiled. His teeth looked like a picket fence in need of whitewashing.

Walter rolled his eyes and sat down in the first row of seats. He looked over the other passengers like a lion picking out a weak zebra from the herd. A homely boy sitting a few seats behind him looked promising.

The boy had big ears, freckles, and a pug nose. His clothes were too big for him, obviously hand-me-downs. There were patches on the knees of his pants. His shoes looked as if they should have been replaced a hundred miles ago.

Walter smirked. *Poor-fect,* he thought.

The boy saw Walter grinning at him and smiled.

Walter nodded and whispered, "Hello, sucker."

"What was that, Wally?" the driver asked.

"Huh? Are you addressing me?"

"Your name is Wally, isn't it?" the driver asked, running his eyes over the passenger list.

"My name is Walter Ridgemont the third," Walter sniffed.

"My missed-stake, Walter," the bus driver cackled. "Fangs for correcting me."

He held the door open while Buffy climbed up the steps onto the bus.

"And this must be your sister, Buffy," the driver said. "I see she's quite the unhappy camper."

"Hmmph," Buffy said, walking past the driver with her nose in the air.

"And so fiendly, too," the driver cackled.

Buffy leaned over and hissed to her brother, "I'm going to get you for this, Walter. You're going to regret this trip."

Walter laughed as she sat beside a skinny girl in shorts and a tank top. He rubbed his hands together. This was going to be so much fun!

The bus driver closed the door and started down the street.

"Hi, I'm Minnie Blunt," said the girl sitting beside Buffy. "But everybody calls me Skinny Minnie. And these are my friends, Darrell and John." She pointed to the boys across the aisle.

"Charmed, I'm sure," Buffy said coldly. "I'm Buffy Ridgemont."

Darrell rested his feet on the back of the seat in front of him. "So why the sour face, Little Miss Moneybags? You don't want to go to Camp Pocahauntus?"

"My mother is making me go," Buffy replied. "It wasn't my idea."

"I know how you feel," Minnie said. "I didn't want to go to camp the first time my mom and dad made me, but you might be surprised. It can be a lot of fun."

"I seriously doubt that," Buffy replied.

"I don't know," Minnie said. "Staying up late. Telling stories. Eating candy…"

John laughed. "Yeah, being away from your parents for a month can be a *real* bummer," he said sarcastically.

Buffy rubbed her chin. "I hadn't thought of that. A whole month of not having to watch my mother give in to my brother's every demand."

"But don't forget," Darrell said, "it's important to make the right friends."

"Yeah, the three of us," John agreed with an evil grin. "We rule Camp Pocahauntus."

"Stick with us," Skinny Minnie added, "and you'll be all right."

Buffy smiled broadly. "You know, maybe camp won't be so bad after all."

She smiled over at Walter, who frowned back.

"So, Walter," the bus driver said. "Is this your fearest trip to Camp Pocahauntus?"

"That's right," Walter replied. "First time."

"I just know you're going to loathe it," the driver cackled. "The camp's built near an Indian burial mound, so there's a local ghost to keep you company at night."

"Oh, right," Walter scoffed. "Who's that?"

"Does the name Crooked Foot Billie wring any necks?" the driver asked.

"No. Should I have heard of him?"

The driver smiled. "Crooked Foot Billie was what the Indians call a shaman, a medicine man. The Seminoles say Crooked Foot cast powerful spells to help his tribe defeat the white men trying to take their land. But one night, a panther came into camp and killed Crooked Foot. Without his magic to protect them, his tribe was defeated. They say his ghost roams the woods looking for revenge against the rich white men who stole his land."

Walter shook his head. "You're just trying to scare me," he said.

"No," the bus driver cackled. "I'm just trying to get you into the fright mood."

The sound of Minnie and her friends laughing interrupted them.

"Sounds like your sister's made some new fiends," the driver said.

"Yes," Walter replied, frowning. *I'll have to do something about that,* he thought.

3
CAMP POCAHAUNTUS

Two hours later, the bus passed through the faded gates of a decrepit Florida fort. A sign that read CAMP POCAHAUNTUS hung crookedly over the entry. Half of the fort walls had collapsed, eaten away by termites.

Inside, the recreation room and the kitchen were dilapidated buildings that looked as if they'd fall over if they even saw a paintbrush. The sleeping quarters were ugly concrete cabins painted to look as if they were constructed of logs. The only building that looked fairly new was the covered picnic area.

The camp counselor, Mr. Smirch, and his old, gray-haired assistant, Ms. Greeble, waited for the bus to stop. The kids in the camp had nicknamed Mr. Smirch "Mr. Lollipop" because of his thin body, big head, and sickly-sweet personality, which was as phony as his hairpiece.

"We have to make a good impression on these Ridgemont kids," Mr. Smirch said to his assistant. "Their parents are very wealthy."

"Wealthy? Hmph," Ms. Greeble said sternly. "Just what we need around here. Some children with a little class."

"Indeed. And if the Ridgemont kids have a good time at Camp Pocahauntus, they'll tell all their rich friends about us. We can get this place fixed up and attract a more sophisticated group of campers, instead of this rabble." He looked down his nose at the campers filing off the bus, carrying their suitcases.

The bus driver leaned out the door. "Goodbye, kiddies. Especially you, Walter. I doubt if you'll have the heart to come back on my bus again. *Heeheeheehee...*"

"What was that supposed to mean?" Walter grumbled as the bus drove away.

"Attention, please!" Ms. Greeble called. "Line up right here in front of Mr. Smirch. On the double!" Ms. Greeble pointed at the ground with an oversize pencil she called "The Camper Corrector."

Walter pushed a smaller kid out of the way

and stood in front of Mr. Smirch. He looked for the jug-eared boy and saw him standing next to Buffy and her new friends.

"Quiet down, campers," Ms. Greeble growled. "Our beloved camp leader, Mr. Smirch, has a few things to say to you."

Darrell leaned over to Buffy. "Ms. Greeble is Mr. Lollipop's enforcer," he whispered. "You have to watch out for her."

"I will," Buffy whispered back.

Ms. Greeble tapped her pencil on the clip-board she carried. "Darrell, perhaps you and your friend need a little reminder of what 'quiet down' means?"

Darrell sneered at her, but kept quiet.

"Go ahead, Mr. Smirch," Ms. Greeble said, casting a baleful eye at Buffy and her friends.

Mr. Smirch smiled and raised his hands. "Welcome, children. Welcome to Camp Pocahauntus," he said, his smile almost touching his ears. "I hope your bus ride was pleasantly pleasing."

"If you like being in an earthquake for two hours," Walter said.

A giggle rippled through the crowd.

Mr. Smirch frowned at Walter. But then he noticed WPR III written on Walter's backpack.

Suddenly, Smirch's frown sprang into a smile. He chuckled as well. "In an earthquake. Oh, that's funny-wunny, Wally."

The young boy frowned. "Walter. The name is Walter Ridgemont the third."

"Of course, Walter, I'm so sorry. I should have known. A boy with your breeding would be a Walter, not a Wally. My mistake."

Mr. Smirch turned to the girl standing next to Walter. "And this must be your sistery-wistery, Buffy. How do you do, young lady?"

"The name's Sally," the little girl said.

Mr. Smirch's grin wavered. "Didn't your sister come with you, Walter?"

"She's way over there," Walter said, pointing to the other end of the line.

Mr. Smirch's grin returned full force. "Hello, Buffy. We're pleased as punch to have you with us at Camp Pocahauntus."

Buffy smiled and whispered something to her new friends. They all giggled.

Walter seethed. Buffy was supposed to be miserable, not all giggly. The trip wasn't starting off quite as he had planned.

"Okely-dokely," Mr. Smirch said. "Now let's get those cabins assigned so you can meet your Pocahauntus pals."

Walter raised his hand.

"Yes, Walter, my boy?"

"Buffy and I want to share a cabin," he said, smiling deviously. That should end his sister's little friendships.

"No!" Buffy cried in surprise. "I don't want to stay with you!"

"She's just kidding," Walter said. "We always stay together. My very wealthy mother insists."

"It's so nice to see a brother and sister get along so well," Mr. Smirch beamed. "However, I'm afraid it's against camp rules for boys and girls to share cabins."

"So change the rules," Walter said, hands on his hips.

Mr. Smirch adjusted his toupee. "Uh, change them, yes, well, um…Ms. Greeble?"

His assistant tapped her clipboard with her pencil. "Against state regulations, sir," she said.

"Ah, there you have it," Smirch said, all smiles. "So sorry, Walter."

Buffy smiled at her brother and stuck out her tongue.

Walter frowned. He wouldn't forget her small victory.

"All right," Walter said. "If that's the case, then I want the cabin behind you."

Mr. Smirch's grin faltered. "Uh, that's my cabin, Walter," he said.

"Well, that's the one I want," Walter said. "It's bigger than the others, and a boy of my stature deserves deluxe accommodations."

A murmur of disapproval rumbled down the line of kids.

Mr. Smirch wiped the sweat from his brow. "Uh, I'm afraid I've already moved all my things in there, Walter my boy. It would be quite a bit of troubley-wubbley to move it all out again."

Mr. Smirch glanced over at his assistant, then started smiling again as he got an idea. "But how about if I assign you the cabin right next door? It's also nice and big."

"But that's *my* cabin!" Ms. Greeble cried, almost dropping her clipboard.

Mr. Smirch patted his assistant on the shoulder. "Now, Ms. Greeble, you haven't moved in yet," he said. "And I'm sure Walter's mother would appreciate you accommodating her son's special needs. Why, she'd probably tell her friends all about it."

"That's true…" Ms. Greeble said, tapping her pencil on her clipboard as she thought it over.

She nodded. "As always, Mr. Smirch, an excellent idea. Besides, it will be easier to keep the brats—er, kids—in line if I stay with them. I'll be glad to let Walter have my cabin."

The other kids stared at Walter. A few mumbled "spoiled brat" and "rotten rich kid."

Mr. Smirch looked down at the camp roster. "Now, for your roommate…"

"I want *him*," Walter said, pointing to the homely boy he had spotted on the bus.

"Ah, Casper Barnes," Smirch said. "Casper, would you like the pleasure of rooming with Walter?"

"Don't do it, Casper," Darrell whispered. "That guy's a real loser."

"Yeah," John said. "He thinks he's a big shot. Stay with us, like you did last year."

"Why? So you can pick on me again?" Casper asked. His backwoods Florida accent was as thick as Key lime pie. "I think maybe I might try a new roommate this summer."

Darrell and John frowned.

"Sure, Mr. Smirch," Casper said with a big grin. "I'll room with Walter."

Walter smiled like a mad scientist who had just received a shipment of lab rats.

"Okay, that's settled," Mr. Smirch said. "Now, Buffy, how about you?"

"I want to stay with Skinny Minnie, way over

there." She pointed at the cabin farthest from Walter's quarters.

"Very well," Mr. Smirch said. "The rest of you, pair up and follow Ms. Greeble. She'll show you to your cabins."

The children got in line behind the assistant counselor.

"Now, we'll meet back here for lunchy-wunchy at twelve o'clock," Mr. Smirch said. "I'll see you then." He started to leave when Walter cleared his throat.

"Mr. Smirch?"

"Yes, Walter?" he asked, all smiles.

"I'm tired from the long trip, and my suitcase and backpack are pretty heavy. Could you get them for me?"

Mr. Smirch's smile faltered. "Carry your bags?"

"Yes," Walter said. "Could you do that for me? I'm sure my Momsy would approve."

"Oh, uh, yes, surely," Mr. Smirch said. He picked up the backpack and suitcase and carried them to Walter's cabin. Casper waited at the door.

The cabin was large, but sparse. A dresser stood next to the bunk bed in one corner of the room. There was a desk and chair in the opposite corner.

Mr. Smirch put Walter's bags on the bottom

bunk and started out the door. "I'll see you boys at lunch."

"Bye, Mr. Smirch," Casper said.

Walter ignored the counselor's exit. He tugged on the front of his shirt. "Whew, it's like a sauna in here. Where's the air conditioner?"

"Ain't one," Casper said, turning on the ceiling fan.

"What?" Walter cried. "No air conditioning?"

"Nope. Guess a rich kid like you got air conditioning in every room of your house. Daddy says we're too poor to afford it. I only get to come to Camp Pocahauntus 'cause of the 'Send a Pauper to Camp' program."

"Look, Casper. I'm not really interested. If you want to do something useful, put my things away. I'll pay you two bucks."

"Two bucks to put your stuff in the dresser? Great!" Casper said, grinning from ear to ear. "My daddy only pays me fifty cents to mow the lawn."

Walter watched as Casper unpacked his bags.

"All done," Casper said after he'd put Walter's clothes in the dresser drawer.

Walter inspected the drawer. "I like my socks on the right side, not the left. Fix it or you don't get paid."

He stood and watched gleefully as Casper rearranged the socks.

"There. All done."

"Good," Walter said. He took two dollar bills from his wallet and held them out for Casper to take. "Here you go."

When Casper reached for the money, Walter let it fall to the ground.

"Oops," Walter said with a smirk.

Casper gathered up the bills and tucked them into his pocket.

Walter grinned. He reached into the drawer and grabbed a handful of socks. He threw them across the room. "I'll give you another dollar if you pick those up."

Casper smiled. "A dollar to pick up some socks? That's a bargain!"

He gathered up the socks and put them back into the drawer.

Walter took out another dollar bill and held it out. Casper reached for it and Walter dropped it again. The bill fluttered under the dresser.

"You sure got slippery fingers, Walter," Casper grunted as he got on his knees and scooped the bill from under the dresser. "Slippery as an eel in a bucket of butter."

Casper snorted a laugh and tucked the bill in

his pocket. "Know something, Walter?" he said. "You're just about the nicest feller I ever met at this here camp. Last year, my roommates, Darrell and John, used to pick on me something awful. And here you are, making a mess just so's you can give me a little spending money."

"What?" Walter cried.

"Aw, I know what you're doing, and I appreciate it. Me being so doggone poor and all."

Walter was speechless. The moron thought he was being nice to him by making him work like a dog for chump change!

Oh, well, thought Walter darkly. *There'll be plenty of chances to show him the error of his ways. Starting with lunch.*

"Come on, Casper," Walter said. "Let's get something to eat."

"All right!" Casper replied. "I'm hungry enough to eat a big old cow."

Good, Walter thought to himself. *Just save room for a double helping of humiliation.*

4
WALTER THE SNAKE HARMER

"This is lunch?" Walter cried. Ms. Greeble had just spooned a ladleful of hot dogs and baked beans onto his plate. "What is this pink-and-brown puke?"

"Beanie-weenies," Ms. Greeble said. "The traditional first meal here at Camp Pocahauntus. High in protein."

"I love 'em," Casper said. "Gimme two scoops."

Ms. Greeble dumped two ladlefuls onto Casper's plate.

Walter wrinkled his nose. "Blecch. They smell disgusting."

"We have hot dogs and beans all the time at home. I just can't get enough," Casper said.

"That just shows how much taste you have," Walter said. "None."

"None. Ha! That's funny, buddy," Casper said, shoveling the beans into his mouth.

"So, Walter, how's your meal?" Mr. Smirch asked as he walked up to the table.

"Meal? You call this swill a meal?" Walter asked, holding up his plate.

"I'm sorry it's not to your liking," Mr. Smirch replied worriedly. "The other kids seem to love the stuff."

From across the table, Darrell snorted a laugh.

"Yeah, right," John added.

"Ask my sister how she likes it, Mr. Smirch," Walter requested. At home, Buffy wouldn't try anything new unless their mother bribed her with candy.

Mr. Smirch swallowed. "Uh, Buffy, how do you like your food?"

Buffy smiled spitefully at her brother. "It's excellent, Mr. Smirch," she said, her tone sickly-sweet. "This is the first time I've ever had hot dogs and beans, and I *love* them." To prove her point, she scooped up a spoonful and choked it down.

"Well, I *hate* them," Walter shouted. He got up, stormed over to the trash compactor, and dumped his plate into it.

Just then, a flicker of movement at his feet

caught his attention. He looked down and began to shake with fear.

"Sn-sn-snuh," Walter stammered, pointing at the ground.

"What is it, Walter?" Mr. Smirch asked.

"Sn-snake! Everybody, look out! It's a snake!"

Mr. Smirch saw a small snake curled up next to the trash compactor.

"Why, that's nothing to be frightened of, my boy," Mr. Smirch said. "Just a rat snake. Perfectly harmless!"

The other kids snickered.

"It—it's a snake!" Walter gasped. "Kill it!"

"Oh, no need for that. These snakes are beneficial. They keep the rats and mice out of the trash compactor."

"I don't care. I want that thing dead. Now!"

"But, Walter…"

"If my mother knew you let snakes slither around, she'd sue your crummy camp into the ground!"

Mr. Smirk straightened his hairpiece. "No need for threats, my boy," he said.

"Then kill that snake! Right now!"

"Um…Ms. Greeble, if you please? A shovel and…" Mr. Smirch made a chopping motion toward the snake.

Ms. Greeble went to get a shovel.

26

Darrell turned to Casper. "Hey, floppy ears, why don't you go save that snake? It's about as ugly as you. Maybe you're related."

"Yeah, Casp," John said. "Ugly is as ugly does."

"Maybe I *will* save the little critter," Casper said stubbornly.

Ms. Greeble returned with the shovel. She stood over the snake, the shovel raised over her head. She brought it down in a fierce swipe, but missed. The frightened reptile bolted toward Walter.

"He's attacking me! Kill it!" Walter screamed, stumbling back against the trash compactor.

Ms. Greeble took another slashing blow at the reptile, but missed again.

"You idiot, he's going to bite me!" Walter cried as the snake raced toward him. "Help!"

Suddenly, Casper stepped in front of the snake and snagged it behind the head. The rat snake coiled around his arm. Casper laughed. "Look, everybody, he's giving me a hug. Guess he must like me."

"Kill that thing!" Walter cried.

"Ain't no reason to kill it, Walter," Casper said. "This snake ain't gonna hurt nobody, are you, little feller?" He stroked the snake on the head, then held it out for Walter to touch. "Go ahead and pet him."

Walter shrank back against the trash compactor.

The other kids laughed.

"Don't be afraid," Casper said, bringing the snake close to Walter again. "Just pet him and you'll see how friendly he is."

Walter was furious. "Keep that thing away from me, you backwoods buffoon! You—you probably have snakes living in your shack with you. Who knows? Your family probably eats them."

Casper's mouth dropped open in surprise.

Walter continued his tirade. "Are you saving that one for dessert after you finish those disgusting beanie-weenies?"

"They ain't no more disgusting than that mean old mouth of yours, Walter. If you ain't careful, I might have to shut it for you."

Walter ignored him. "Or maybe you want the snake to catch a rat for you. That's probably your favorite meal."

"Now, Walter, my boy," Mr. Smirch said. "Casper was only trying to help—in his own way."

"I don't need any help from this smelly oaf," Walter said. "Unless I want my gutter cleaned or the trash taken out."

He reached into his pocket and pulled out a dollar bill. "Here, Casper. I'll give you a dollar to show us how you eat snake meat."

"How about I give *you* the snake to eat!" Casper said, tossing the snake at Walter. Walter shrieked and threw up his hands. The snake landed at Walter's feet and tried to escape. But before it could, the enraged Walter stomped on its head with the hard sole of his hiking boot.

Casper let out an anguished cry. "Now look what I done! My daddy told me to control my temper. Now I've gone and let you kill that nice old snake!"

He picked it up and looked at it sorrowfully. "I got to give you a proper burial, Mr. Snake," he said. "Seeing that it's all my fault for letting that rotten Walter kill you."

He carried the snake toward the woods.

"You're not fooling anybody," Walter called after him. "You just don't want to share your dessert!"

Suddenly, a scream rang out from the forest.

Everyone took off running to see what had happened.

When they saw Casper, several kids screamed.

Casper had stepped into a poacher's trap. His leg was bent at a painful angle. Blood oozed down his pants.

"My leg. It hurts bad," Casper moaned.

Mr. Smirch stepped forward. "Take it easy, Casper," he said. "I'll get you out of there."

He turned to Ms. Greeble. "Um, Ms. Greeble... would you mind?"

She sighed, then grabbed the jaws of the trap and pried them open. Gingerly, she pulled Casper's mangled leg out of the trap.

Darrell, John, Minnie, and Buffy walked over to Walter. Darrell grabbed Walter by the shirt.

"Casper was our favorite kid to pick on, but now you've ruined our fun. I guess we're gonna have to pick on somebody else."

"Yeah," John said, poking Walter with his finger. "Somebody like a rich kid with a big mouth and a bad attitude."

"Know anybody like that, Buffy?" Minnie asked.

"I might know one especially rotten rich kid," Buffy said, grinning.

Walter shook himself free of Darrell's grasp.

"If you think you can scare me, you're wrong," he growled, backing away from them. "Dead wrong. Nobody gets the better of Walter Ridgemont the third. And anybody that tries is going to regret it!"

Walter turned and headed for his cabin.

"We'll see about that, rich boy," Darrell said ominously. "We'll just see."

5
A SNAKE IN THE GROSS

A chorus of birds sang the praises of a new morning. The sun glistened on the dew on the grass. Squirrels jumped from branch to branch in the pine trees behind the cabins.

Inside his cabin, Walter chuckled in his sleep. He was having a wonderful dream. In it, a giant snake wrapped its coils around his former roommate.

"How do you like your hug, Casper?" Walter asked as the snake squeezed the life out of the poor boy. Casper's face turned purple and his eyes bulged.

The python unhinged its jaw and began to swallow Casper headfirst. It gulped him down inch by inch. Soon the snake had a bulge in its body the size of a small boy.

31

"I thought you said snakes were friendly," Walter chortled.

The smile froze on his face when the snake turned its head and grinned at him. Its eyes burned with a fiery red glow. Walter gasped when he realized that the snake had Casper's face.

"This snake ain't gonna hurt nobody," Casper the Friendly Snake said. His grin exposed his sharp, curved teeth. "Well, maybe just *one* person."

Walter tried to move away from the snake, but his legs felt weak and shaky.

Casper slithered toward him. His gleaming red eyes watched Walter's every move.

"Stay back!" Walter cried as he desperately tried to get away. His legs wouldn't respond.

Casper kept coming. The raspy hiss of his scales along the ground filled Walter with horror.

"Don't worry, Walter. I just want to give you a little hug." The snake's laugh was a hissing nightmare that sent a shudder rippling up Walter's spine.

"I'll give you a thousand dollars to leave me alone!" Walter shouted. "Two thousand!"

"Now, what good is money to a snake, Walter?" Casper chuckled. "You, on the other hand, would make a nice meal. Kinda like the rats you said I liked to eat!" The smile dropped off the snake's face. His red eyes burned with the fires of vengeance.

Walter turned away and felt the snake's cold, smooth scales slide against his cheek. He screamed and opened his eyes.

Suddenly, he realized there really *was* something cool and slick against his cheek!

Walter's shriek ripped through the serenity of the camp. The birds flew off. The squirrels scampered to the highest branches.

"A snake!" Walter screamed as he hurled the reptile's body across the room. Banging his head on the top bunk, Walter jumped from the bed and ran out of the cabin.

"There's a snake in my room!" he shrieked. "There's a snake in my…"

Suddenly, sharp pains racked his shins and feet as he tripped over a stack of fallen branches.

"What the…" he cried. He fell toward a soupy brown puddle. "Oh, no!"

Walter fell face-first into the mud puddle. The squishy brown earth went up his nose and into his mouth. His silk pajamas were ruined.

He snorted the mud from his nose and spit it out of his mouth.

He lay in the puddle for a moment, too

stunned to move. How had the branches gotten there? And where had that puddle come from? It hadn't rained the night before.

Then he became aware of laughter.

Wiping the mud from his eyes, Walter looked up and saw Buffy laughing at him, along with Minnie, Darrell, and John.

"Having a bad morning, Wally by Golly?" Buffy asked.

The four of them laughed.

"You all did this?" Walter asked, seething.

"Put that snake you killed in your bed, yes," Buffy giggled. "It was Darrell's idea."

"I thought you might like a little company, since your roommate had to leave camp early," Darrell said. He tossed away the water hose he'd used to make the puddle.

"Yeah, we thought you might get lonely," John added.

They all laughed.

Walter's face got red.

"What's wrong, Wally by Golly? Mommy not here to protect you?" Buffy asked.

Walter wiped more mud off his face. "You shouldn't have done it," he said, gritting his teeth. "I could've had a heart attack!"

The kids laughed.

"You shouldn't have dared us to mess with you," Skinny Minnie said. "Now you're just gonna get more and more abuse."

"Because we rule this camp," John said. "And we don't like rich brats like you messing things up."

Walter stared at them. The mud dripped from his face.

"Come on, guys," Darrell said. "Let's go get breakfast. Making rich kids look like dorks really works up my appetite."

"See you there, Wally by Golly," Buffy gloated. "Unless, of course, you're full from eating all those mud pies." She and her friends snickered.

Walter watched the foursome walk back toward their cabins. "I'll get you back for this," he growled. "Even if it costs me an arm and a leg, I'll get my revenge!"

6
BUY ONE, GUT ONE FREE

"Try the serve again, my boy," Mr. Smirch said, tossing the volleyball back to Walter.

It had been a week since the snake incident. In that time, Walter had become an object of ridicule at Camp Pocahauntus.

Buffy and her friends made fun of him at every opportunity, much to the delight of the other campers. Whenever he tried to flaunt his wealth, Buffy, Minnie, Darrell, and John would cut him down to size. He felt lower than a wad of gum on someone's shoe.

Walter stood at the service line of the volleyball court. He stamped his foot. "This stinks," he grumbled.

"Come on, my boy, give it another try," Mr. Smirch said.

"I hate this game," Walter said.

"The only way to get better is to practice, practice, practice!" Mr. Smirch replied cheerfully. "Now go ahead and serve it."

Walter threw the ball up and took a swipe at it. He missed it entirely, and the white ball knocked off his cap.

The kids exploded in laughter. Walter's ears burned red.

"That's using your head, Wally by Golly," Darrell called.

Walter kicked the ball into the bushes and ran to his cabin.

"Walter, come back here," Mr. Smirch said.

Walter opened the door to his cabin, went inside, and slammed the door.

"Those stupid morons, they'll pay for making fun of Walter Ridgemont the third," he said as tears came to his eyes. "I swear it."

Walter stayed in his cabin for most of the afternoon until Mr. Smirch announced over the PA system that it was time for arts and crafts.

Walter sniffed. "Count me out, Lollipop. I won't be there." He got up from his bunk and went outside.

Buffy, Minnie, Darrell, and John were walking past his cabin on their way to the rec room.

"Oh, look! It's my brother, the jock," Buffy said.

"Oooh, my hero!" Minnie said, acting as if she might faint. "Can I have your autograph?" she snickered.

Walter looked away and walked faster.

"Hey, you guys," John said, winking at his friends. "Want to play Wally-by-Gollyball?"

"How do you play that, John?" Darrell asked, laughing.

John smiled. "It's easy. You just throw the ball up and let it hit you in the head."

They all laughed.

Walter hurried for the safety of the woods. "I'll get them back," he promised himself. "Somehow."

The sun sliced into the shadows cast by the large oak and pine trees. A trail wound its way through the streaks of light. Aluminum plates nailed to the pine trees marked the trail.

"How can they make fun of me?" Walter mumbled, heading down the trail. "I just don't get it. I'm so much better than they are."

The dense woods trapped the heat of the afternoon sun. Walter wiped the sweat from his forehead with the sleeve of his shirt. Suddenly, he tripped over the knobby root of a cypress tree, falling down and scuffing his hands.

"Stupid woods," Walter said, struggling to his

feet. He rubbed his aching toe.

Ahead of him, an armadillo foraged for food. Walter picked up a clump of black dirt and hit the animal with it. The armadillo scurried into the bushes.

Walter laughed and felt a little better.

Over to his left, he saw a clearing and went to investigate. It was a sinkhole that dropped straight down a long way. Chunks of rock littered the pit's floor.

"Whew. I'd hate to be out here at night and fall into that," Walter said, looking over the edge of the pit.

He returned to the trail and continued his trip into the woods.

"Stupid jerks picking on me," he grumbled, looking down at the ground. "Who do they think they are?"

As he ventured deeper down the trail, the thickening undergrowth obscured the pie-plate trail markers. Palmetto bushes and scrub oaks clawed into the path, making it difficult to follow.

"I'm Walter Ridgemont the third," he said. "I could buy and sell all of them. Those…"

Walter stopped and looked around.

He suddenly realized that he had lost sight of the pie-plate markers. He spun around, trying to find the trail, but couldn't locate it. A slithery snake of panic squeezed his insides.

"Stay calm, Walter," he said. "You're not lost."

He looked up into the sky to try and get his bearings by using the sun. The covering of trees obscured it. The snake of panic returned, slithering up his spine and sending goose bumps flying up and down his arms.

Then he thought he heard something moving through the woods.

"Hello?" Walter called out.

There was no answer.

Only the rustling of leaves.

Walter's heart thumped against his ribs like a caged gorilla. Beads of nervous perspiration popped onto his face.

The thing in the woods moved again. Leaves crackled underfoot. Branches snapped. Whatever it was, it was *big*.

And it was getting closer.

Walter picked up a pine branch as a weapon. The rotten wood crumbled in his hand.

The thing kept coming.

The hair on the back of his neck stood on end. He tried to cry out to scare away the creature, but his voice caught in his throat.

The bushes rattled nearby.

Walter turned to run.

But the thing was there! A huge monster with a skull in the middle of its chest.

Walter covered his head with his arms and screamed.

"Quiet, boy," the thing said.

Walter opened one eye, then the other.

He saw that the thing was not a monster, it was a man. An Indian. The Indian wore the bright patchwork shirt, scarf, and blue jeans of the Seminole tribe. A turban with one feather sticking from the side adorned the Seminole's white-haired head. The skull Walter had seen growing from the monster's chest was that of a raccoon dangling from a leather necklace.

"You're not a monster," Walter said.

"No, I'm a Seminole," the big man said. "Now, what are you doing out here, boy?"

"I, uh, came out to do some thinking and got lost," Walter said. "Can you help me?"

"Does the moon help the panther to see his prey at night?" the Indian asked. "Do the wings of a bird help it fly?"

"Is that a yes?" Walter asked.

The Indian nodded. "You say you came to the woods to do some thinking."

"Yes, and I got lost."

The Indian nodded. "You lost your way because thoughts of revenge clouded your mind."

Walter's mouth dropped open. "How did you know?"

"I sense a need for vengeance in you, boy," the Indian said. "It radiates out from you like ripples on water. Who has done you this wrong?"

"My little rat sister and her seedy friends at Camp Pocahauntus," Walter sniffed.

"And you desire revenge against them?"

"Yes."

"Come with me," the Indian said.

"Wait a minute," Walter replied. "Where are we going?"

"To my chickee."

"Chickee?"

"My home. There I will give you the means for your revenge. But I warn you, it carries a heavy cost."

"I don't care what it costs. Money is no object. Momsy will send me whatever I want."

The Indian smiled a secret smile. "Very well. Come, then. It is not far from here."

The Indian led Walter deeper into the woods until they came to his chickee. It was a thatched hut, with six poles holding up the woven-palm-frond roof and no walls.

"This is where you live?"

The Indian nodded. "We have much to do."

They entered the hut. Although it had no walls, the inside of the chickee was unusually dark, as though the sun was afraid to enter.

Walter sat down in front of a smoldering campfire.

"I'm Walter Ridgemont the third. What's your name?" Walter asked the big Indian.

"I have many names. White men call me Crazy Panther. I am called shaman by my people. Crooked Foot Billie is the name given to me by my father."

"Crooked Foot Billie," Walter mumbled to himself. Where had he heard that name before?

Crooked Foot sat in front of the campfire and removed a sharp knife from a sheath on his belt. He tested the blade with his thumb and smiled at Walter.

Walter felt a nervous tickle in his belly. "Sharp, huh?" he said, trying to keep the smile on his face.

Suddenly, horror engulfed Walter as he realized where he'd heard the Indian's name before. He started to tremble. Crooked Foot was the ghost the bus driver had told him about, the one who killed rich white men!

His eyes bulged with terror as the Indian

reached for him, his sinewy fingers clutching like talons.

"Oh, no," Walter cried. "I'm gonna be scalped!" He closed his eyes and waited for the blade to strike.

A sudden pain stabbed his head as Crooked Foot plucked one of his hairs.

Walter opened his eyes and watched Crooked Foot split the hair with the knife edge.

"One hair makes a poor scalp," Crooked Foot said. "I just wanted to show you that the blade of my knife is as sharp as the claws of the bobcat."

Walter let out his breath. *That stupid bus driver,* he thought, *he must have known this Indian lives out here in the woods. He told me that story to scare me if I ran into him.*

In the glow of the smoldering campfire, Crooked Foot removed a small piece of cypress wood from a pouch he carried. Using the knife, he began to carve the wood.

Walter watched the Indian's nimble blade nick and sculpt the wood. Slowly, the cypress chunk began to take shape.

When Crooked Foot was through, he dipped the carving into a bowl of oils. He took it out and rubbed it with a rabbitskin.

"Can I see…"

"Quiet!" Crooked Foot said. "They must hear my words."

"Who must hear your words?"

Crooked Foot put a rough finger against Walter's lips. "Shh. You need not worry."

He wrapped the carving in a bed of palmetto fronds.

The old Indian began to chant over the carving. His words soared into the air and through the forest.

Walter rolled his eyes. What was this guy trying to pull with the phony ritual stuff? Walter had hoped the Indian would give him some kind of poison made from the bark of a tree or something. If Crooked Foot thought he was going to be paid for all this mumbo-jumbo, he *was* a Crazy Panther.

Crooked Foot increased the tempo of his chant, then suddenly stopped.

"It is done," he said. Beads of sweat dripped from his forehead. He held up the carving, which Walter could now see was of an eagle. The Indian removed a long cord of rawhide from the pouch and pulled it through a ring carved at the top of the eagle's head. He handed Walter the necklace.

"What am I supposed to do with this?" Walter asked incredulously.

45

Crooked Foot smiled. "That is an animal-spirit totem. Whoever wears the totem for one day will act just like the animal the totem represents on the following day."

"No way," Walter cried.

Crooked Foot nodded. "Yes, boy. The magic is strong."

Suddenly dozens of possibilities sprang into Walter's mind, all of them nasty. "Look, maybe your magic is strong," he said, "but I'm no sucker. I'm not paying for anything until I see if it works."

The Indian smiled and said, "No one ever pays until *after* the totem performs its magic."

Walter nodded. "You can bet on that."

Crooked Foot pointed out of the chickee. "Go! Your time with me is over."

"But I don't know how to get back to camp," Walter protested.

The Indian whistled shrilly.

A scruffy dog ran into the chickee. Crooked Foot said a few Indian words to the mongrel.

"My dog will lead you to the camp," Crooked Foot said.

"Your *dog?*"

"Go!" Crooked Foot commanded. "I will speak no more." He folded his arms and closed his eyes.

Walter shrugged and tucked the eagle totem

into his shirt pocket. He turned and followed the dog into the woods.

Twenty minutes later, he arrived on the outskirts of Camp Pocahauntus.

"Well, how do you like that," Walter said. "It looks like you know— Hey! Where'd he go?"

The dog had vanished.

For a chilling moment, Walter had the creepy feeling that he had, in fact, encountered a ghost. He reached up and felt the eagle totem in his pocket. No, Crooked Foot was real. As real as the totem. He smiled.

His smile broadened when he saw Darrell walking across the campgrounds. The boy carried a trash bag toward the compactor.

Walter approached him.

"Well, if it isn't Jerky Jock," Darrell said. "How about a game of catch?"

He threw the trash bag at Walter. It hit him in the chest and split open. Smelly garbage spilled onto his shoes.

Darrell guffawed.

Walter shook a black banana peel off his foot and said, "I was going to give you a peace offering, but now…"

"Who says I want to make peace?" Darrell said. "But if I did, what were you going to give me?"

Walter reached into his pocket and pulled out the eagle totem necklace. "This."

Darrell raised his eyebrows. "Pretty cool," he said, admiring the realistic carving.

Suddenly, he snatched the necklace out of Walter's hands. "But who needs to make peace? I'll just take this and keep messing with you anyway. That's more fun."

"Give it back," Walter said, putting on a show of mock protest.

Darrell slipped the necklace over his head. "Sorry, rich boy. I don't think so." He admired the carving. "The great thing is, I get this for free. I don't have to pay you a thing!"

He laughed and strutted back toward his cabin.

"Oh, don't worry," Walter said. An evil grin crept across his face. "You'll pay for the necklace tomorrow morning. You'll pay in full!"

7
A BIRD IN THE HEAD

The alarm clock by the side of Walter's bed clattered a wake-up call. Walter slapped it dead with a swat of his hand. He opened one eye, and it was promptly stabbed by a shaft of sunlight. He closed the eye and rolled over in bed.

Suddenly, he remembered why he'd wanted to wake up so early. He sat up in bed, swung his legs over the bunk, and put on his slippers.

"It's showtime!" Walter crowed.

He dressed quickly and stepped out of the cabin.

"Rise and shine, Darrell," he chuckled. "The early bird gets the worm."

He found a spot in the woods just outside Darrell's cabin. Peering from behind a palmetto bush, he waited for Darrell to appear.

The humid morning air was like a smothering blanket. Mosquitoes buzzed around his head. He slapped at them.

"Come on, Darrell," Walter whispered, glancing at his watch. "Any time now."

Darrell's cabin door remained closed.

Walter was starting to doubt the power of the totem when all of a sudden the cabin door burst open. The high-pitched screech of an eagle echoed across the campground.

"Ah, here comes old Eagle Beak now," Walter said as he hunkered down behind the bushes to watch.

Darrell ran out of the cabin. He screeched again, flapping his arms wildly.

"I better get closer if I want a bird's-eye view of the fun," Walter cackled as he moved behind another bush.

Darrell jumped up onto a bench and looked around the campgrounds. He turned his head sharply when a movement caught his eye. It was a squirrel hopping across the grounds in search of a meal.

Walter spotted the squirrel. "Oh, good, Darrell won't miss breakfast," he chuckled. "It wouldn't be fair if he did, and I'm all for eagle rights."

Darrell waited for the unwary squirrel to

approach the bench. His eyes were fixed on the hopping animal.

Closer and closer the squirrel moved.

Darrell coiled into a crouch.

Closer. Almost within reach.

Walter shivered in anticipation.

Closer.

Darrell flapped his arms to take flight. He pounced on the rodent, using his bare feet as if they were talons. The squirrel squealed once as Darrell landed on it with his full weight.

Darrell screeched in triumph. He scooped the dead animal up with his toes and dropped it onto the picnic table. He began to tear at it with his teeth.

"I didn't know Darrell liked his meat so rare," Walter chortled.

After Darrell finished devouring half the squirrel, he flapped his arms and took off running into the woods.

"Now where's he going?" Walter wondered aloud as he chased after the eagle boy.

Down the trail Darrell flew, with Walter in hot pursuit.

Suddenly, a rabbit darted across the trail. Darrell gave chase, veering off and heading for a clearing. Walter recognized it from his trip into the woods the day before. It was the clearing where the sinkhole was located!

Darrell headed straight for the deep hole, waving his arms and screaming like an eagle.

Walter stopped and watched him.

As he reached the edge of the sinkhole, Darrell jumped into the air, trying to take flight. He dropped like a stone, still flapping and screeching like the bird he thought he was. He hit the rocks with a sickening *thump*.

Walter ran to the edge of the chasm and peered down. It was a grisly sight.

Walter shook his head. "I warned you not to mess with me, Darrell," he said darkly. "Now I'm going to teach Buffy and the others the same lesson. All I need is three more totems."

After a last look down into the sinkhole, Walter turned and headed off into the woods. He hoped he could remember where Crooked Foot's chickee was located.

But Walter was no woodsman, and he soon became lost again. He turned in a circle, trying to get his bearings. The trees around him all looked the same. A mockingbird chattered a laugh. Walter picked up a fallen branch and hurled it at the bird.

"Shut up, you filthy bag of feathers," Walter called.

"You shouldn't talk to the animals like that," said a voice from behind him.

Walter jumped about three feet. He turned and saw Crooked Foot standing in the woods, his arms folded, the mysterious smile on his face. He seemed to have appeared from out of nowhere.

"Boy, am I glad to see you, Crooked Foot," Walter said.

"Yes, being lost in the woods can be a frightening thing," Crooked Foot said.

"I'm not talking about that," Walter said. "I would eventually have found my way to your chickee."

Crooked Foot's smile looked doubtful. "Your eyes tell me you have seen the power of the totem," the Indian said.

"Yeah," Walter said with an evil grin. "It was amazing."

"So you have come to pay?"

"No. I mean, I'll pay if you want," Walter said. "But the reason I came was to buy three more totems."

"Your thirst for revenge is a well that cannot be filled," the Indian said. "Come, we shall go create them. But I must tell you, the forest mother will only free the spirit of one of her children at a time."

"So only one person can be possessed by a

totem in one day?" Walter asked.

"Yes."

"But the next day, another one will be possessed, right?"

"That is true."

Walter's grin was pure evil. "Let's do it."

Crooked Foot moved swiftly through the woods. Although he was a large man, Crooked Foot didn't ruffle even the smallest of leaves. While Walter left footprints in the soft earth of the trail, the Indian left none. He moved like the wind blowing through the trees.

How does he do that? Walter wondered as he battered his way through the bushes, attempting to keep up with the Indian. His clumsy footsteps were loud enough to wake a hibernating bear.

"Must be some stupid Indian trick," he mumbled. "Walking without making noise."

Crooked Foot moved onto a thin trail of trampled grass. He turned and motioned to Walter. "Come. The path of the deer shows us the way."

Walter wiped the sweat from his eyes. "Path of the deer, my foot. Why can't somebody build a highway through these stupid woods?"

Crooked Foot turned and started down the path. The narrow trail bent sharply to the left, and the Indian disappeared from view.

Walter hurried after him. When he turned at the bend, he ran into a huge spider web that stretched across the trail. The resident banana spider landed on him and raced up his neck. Its three-inch legs carried it quickly onto the side of his face.

"Aaah!" he screamed, slapping the arachnid. He crushed the spider, spraying yellow goo across his face. "Gross!"

Walter wiped his face with his shirt. He looked back at the tattered web.

How did Crooked Foot make it down the trail without disturbing that giant web? he wondered.

"Another stupid Indian trick," he muttered.

"Come!" Crooked Foot shouted, fifty feet down the trail. "It is not far."

Walter wiped his sticky palm on his pants leg. "Give me a second, will you!" he huffed.

Crooked Foot moved away from him and vanished into a stand of pine trees.

"Slow down, you idiotic Indian," Walter grumbled as he jogged toward the spot where Crooked Foot had disappeared. His face was sticky with spider guts and sweat. He looked on the ground for a footprint to see which way Crooked Foot went. He saw none. "How can he move so fast without even making a mark on the ground?"

Walter pushed past a palmetto bush, scratching his arm, and stepped into a small clearing.

"Stupid bushes," Walter grumbled, rubbing the scratch. He looked around the woods. "Crooked Foot, where are you?"

Walter heard rustling behind him. He turned around and saw a black snake slithering among the dead branches.

"Aaah!" he screamed. He turned and ran straight into Crooked Foot.

Walter jumped back. "Don't sneak up on me like that!" he shouted.

Crooked Foot smiled. "We are here."

Walter looked around him. "Are you sure we're not lost?" he complained. "I don't remember any of this."

Crooked Foot parted a thick stand of bushes and revealed his chickee. "We are home."

"It's about time," Walter said, wiping the sweat from his brow. His forearm stung where the thorny branch had clawed it.

The two went into the chickee and sat beside the smoldering campfire. Crooked Foot removed a piece of cypress wood from a bag hanging on a pole. He took out his knife and began to carve the wood.

Walter watched, tapping his foot impatiently.

Slowly, an animal began to take shape.

Crooked Foot raised his head and closed his eyes. He carved the wood expertly, despite the fact that he never looked down. The blade nimbly sliced the cypress as though it had a life of its own.

Soon a pile of wood chips gathered at the Seminole's feet. He placed the finished totem in the bowl of oil.

"Can I see it?" Walter asked.

"You must wait for all three to be completed," Crooked Foot said. He grabbed another piece of wood and began the second animal.

Soon all three were ready. He placed them in the sacred oils.

Crooked Foot removed the finished totems from the bowl and rubbed them with the soft rabbitskin. His eyes rolled back into his head, and he began to chant the spell of possession.

Walter licked his lips in greedy anticipation.

The chickee filled with the sound of the Indian's mournful voice. His words once again seemed to float and vanish as though carried off by a strange wind.

"It is done," Crooked Foot said. His eyes returned to normal again.

"Let me see them," Walter said, reaching for the totems.

Crooked Foot handed him the lifelike carvings.

The first totem was a boar. Fearsome tusks jutted from the corners of its mouth. Its eyes seemed to watch Walter. The second totem was an alligator, with a gaping mouth full of jagged teeth. The gator's wooden hide felt rough to the touch. The third totem was a raccoon. Its open jaws revealed sharp fangs.

"Wow, these are amazing," Walter breathed. "This raccoon looks like it might bite me. How did you carve these little teeth so fast?"

"It is a gift," Crooked Foot said. "But the totem is not."

"I know, I know. You want your payment," Walter said, reaching for his wallet.

Crooked Foot raised his hand. "No," he said. "Not until all of our business is concluded. I just wanted to remind you that you *will* have to pay for using the spirits of the animals."

"Oh, sure," Walter said, gluing a virtuous smile to his face. Inside, he was delighted. Now that he had what he wanted, he had no intention of paying Crooked Foot. Why should he? If the Seminole was dumb enough to give him the totems on credit, let him get stiffed.

"Go now," Crooked Foot said.

Walter looked out at the thick snarl of woods. "Uh, Crooked Foot?"

Crooked Foot motioned toward the door. "The dog will lead you."

As if by magic, the scruffy mongrel that had guided Walter back to camp the first time reappeared.

"Take the boy home," Crooked Foot said.

The dog barked once and waited for Walter to join him.

"I'll see you soon," Walter lied.

Crooked Foot smiled. "Sooner than you think," he said.

The dog led Walter back to camp and then vanished into the brush.

"Thanks again, mutt," Walter said as he followed the trail back into camp. He walked across the grounds past Mr. Smirch's cabin. The counselor was just coming out.

"Oh, there you are, my boy," Mr. Smirch said. "Been out for a little hike? Stretching the old leggy-weggies?"

"Sure," Walter replied.

"You didn't happen to see Darrell out there, did you?"

"Darrell?" Walter replied innocently. "Why, no, sir. Is he missing?"

"His roommate, John, said Darrell was gone when he woke up. And we haven't been able to find him."

Walter stifled a grin. "Maybe he took off. Or maybe he just decided to take a break." *A body break,* he thought gleefully.

Mr. Smirch smoothed his toupee. "Ms. Greeble and I are going to form a couple of search parties to comb the woods."

"Can I come?" Walter asked. "I just can't bear the thought of Darrell wandering around lost in those woods. Who knows what might happen to him out there?"

Mr. Smirch smiled. "Well, well, I'm pleased as punch that you feel that way. Yes, indeed. Such a generous boy you are, Walter. So giving."

"I just want to help, like any good camper would, Mr. Smirch."

Mr. Smirch patted Walter on the head. "Such an unselfish attitude."

"I learned it from you, Mr. Smirch," Walter said.

Mr. Smirch's smile got even bigger. "Yes, well, we do try to teach values here at Camp Pocahauntus. Perhaps you could put in a good word with your mother about us?"

"Maybe," Walter replied coyly. He wanted to make Smirch squirm a little.

"Yes, well, that's all I can ask for," Mr. Smirch said, clearing his throat. "So, anyway, back to poor Darrell. We're meeting at the picnic tables in five minutes to start the search."

"I'll be there."

Mr. Smirch started toward the picnic area, then stopped abruptly. "Oh, Walter, I want all the children to keep an eye out for a bobcat. We found a half-eaten squirrel near the eastern cabins."

"I'll watch the area with an eagle eye," Walter said, then coughed to disguise his laughter.

"Do that," Smirch said. "I'll see you in five minutes."

Walter made it back to his cabin before bursting out with laughter. "A bobcat?" he squealed. "An eagle ate that squirrel, Mr. Lollipop. An eagle that couldn't fly too well."

He chuckled as he removed the three necklaces from his pocket. "And now I have a feeling that the camp is going to become even more beastly."

After he changed his spider-stained shirt, Walter joined the others at the picnic area. He had gifts to give a certain trio of kids.

John, Minnie, and Buffy stood together.

"What's the big deal?" John said. "Darrell's only been gone for a few hours."

"Yeah," Skinny Minnie said. "I'd rather be playing volleyball."

Buffy nodded. "I seriously doubt that Darrell's lost. We should be having fun instead of marching through the dumb woods."

Mr. Smirch stood on the bench of a picnic table and addressed the group. "Okay, kiddiewiddies," he said. "We're going to form into groups of ten. Ms. Greeble will lead one group, and I will lead the other."

Ms. Greeble rapped her pencil on the clipboard. "Let's move it!"

Walter joined John, Minnie, and his sister's group. Mr. Smirch was their leader.

"I can't believe you're going to help," Buffy said to her brother. "I thought you'd be off somewhere counting your money."

"Look," Walter said, "didn't Darrell tell you we buried the hatchet? We're friends now."

"Yeah, right," John sneered. "Darrell said you wanted to make friends. But he brushed you off and took that cool necklace you tried to bribe him with."

Walter removed the totem necklaces from his pocket and held them up. "You mean like these?"

John snatched them out of his hand. "Yeah, just like these."

"Give them back," Walter whined, trying not to smirk.

"You want them?" John said. "Here!"

Walter reached for the necklaces, but John pulled them away. "Now, now! Don't get grabby, Wally. It isn't polite!"

"But those are mine!" Walter pleaded.

"Here," John said. "I'll give you the pig one back."

As Walter reached for it, John tossed it to Minnie. She laughed and slipped it over her head.

"Oops, I missed," John said. "Here. You can have the alligator back."

Walter halfheartedly snatched at the alligator carving as John flipped it to Buffy.

"Oh, it's so chic," Buffy giggled as she put on the necklace.

John looked at the two girls and shook his head. "Now the girls and Darrell all have these cool necklaces, but I still don't. Guess I'll have to keep the raccoon to make things even."

He slipped the necklace over his head.

Walter stamped his foot. "That's not fair," he cried, struggling not to laugh out loud.

"No, it's not," Buffy sneered. "But Mother's not here to take your side, so you'll have to live with it. Ha!" She laughed in Walter's face.

"I guess you win," Walter said, pretending defeat. But inside he was thinking, *Perfect!*

"All right, kids," Mr. Smirch said. "Let's begin the search. Keep your eyes open and, if you find anything, just give a little shout."

An hour later, John's screams tore through the woods.

He had found Darrell.

That night, gloom hung over the camp like a cloud of toxic fog. No one spoke. There was no music. There was no sound at all except for the steady chirping of the crickets and an occasional sob from Mr. Smirch, who'd just discovered that the camp didn't have accident insurance.

Walter couldn't sleep. He kept cackling with glee. He tossed and turned in the bunk bed. Who would be the next victim to take a walk on the wild side? Would it be Buffy the Alligator? John the Raccoon? Or maybe Skinny Minnie the Wild Pig?

He smiled and closed his eyes.

"So who's it going to be?" he whispered. "Who will be the next victim?"

8
A MASHING SUCCESS

Walter woke up moments before the alarm went off. He climbed out of bed, got dressed, and went outside. He found a spot where he could watch both John's and the girls' cabins, since he didn't know which of them would be the first to be affected.

Walter looked at his watch. It was a little past six. The sun was just beginning to peek over the horizon and slice into the foggy mist that shrouded the camp.

"Almost time for the creature feature," Walter whispered.

The minutes flowed past like mud through an hourglass. A turkey buzzard circled the camp in a lazy glide. Walter's legs began to cramp from crouching in the bushes.

Still…

No one left the cabins.

"Where are they?" Walter mumbled.

The sun climbed into the sky, ripping the misty shroud into patchy fog. A horsefly buzzed Walter's head, looking for a tasty spot of flesh. Walter rubbed his aching calves.

And still…

No one came out.

"This is ridiculous," Walter muttered. "If that Indian's magic doesn't work, I'm…"

Nearby, Walter heard the rustling of plastic, then the sound of a paper bag being torn. He crouched down and waddled over to a fallen log to get a better view.

A grin slithered onto his face. It was John!

He was rummaging through the refuse in the trash compactor. The possessed boy had his hands pulled up to his chest like paws. He chattered noisily as he rummaged through the garbage.

"Of course," Walter said, snapping his fingers. "I should have known. Raccoons are nocturnal. John went wild sometime last night."

John ripped open a plastic garbage bag with his teeth. A foul-smelling pile of chicken bones spilled out onto the trash heap. Barbecued chicken had been the main course three nights ago.

"Oh, that is so *fowl*," Walter giggled.

John pawed through the trash, then picked up a half-eaten chicken leg. He rubbed his hands together, the way a raccoon does before it eats.

"Mmm," Walter cackled. "Finger-licking good."

John ate the decaying flesh on the chicken leg, then dropped the bone into the trash. He rummaged through the bag and located a paper plate with two-day-old spaghetti clinging to it. John began to lick and gnaw at the crusty spaghetti.

"I guess John just couldn't *pasta* up the spaghetti," Walter snickered.

After John ate the crusty pasta and part of the paper plate, he dug deeper into the trash compactor. His head was barely visible as he foraged through the garbage.

Then Walter heard footsteps approaching. He lay flat on the ground.

John must also have heard the footsteps. Believing himself to be a raccoon, he dug deeper in the compactor, hiding from whoever was coming.

It was Mr. Smirch, carrying a bag of trash. He lightly tossed the bag on top of the pile and walked over to the switch that activated the compactor.

Mr. Smirch doesn't know John's in there, and John can't tell him, Walter thought with a sinister smile. "What's the matter, John?" he whispered. "Raccoon got your tongue?"

Mr. Smirch flipped the switch on the trash compactor. The machine hummed to life, coughed a black puff of smoke, and began to crush the garbage.

Mr. Smirch walked back to his cabin, whistling a happy tune.

Walter heard the frantic chattering of the raccoon boy as he tried to climb out of the trap.

But it was too late.

The metal walls of the compactor squeezed the garbage in around him. A sound like the snapping of twigs crackled from inside the bin.

The compactor finished its grisly task and opened. Walter looked around. Did he dare risk a peek?

"Does a bear live in the woods?" Walter giggled. He hurried to the side of the compactor and peered over the lip of one side.

"Uh-oh, John," Walter cackled at the ugly sight. "Looks like you had a little too much squash!"

Two down, two to go, he thought maliciously as he hurried back to his cabin to get ready for breakfast.

All of the kids sat at the covered picnic area and waited for Ms. Greeble to put the food on the table.

Walter joined his sister and Minnie at their table. He smiled when he saw the totem necklaces around their necks.

"Where's John?" Walter asked, knowing full well where he was. "In his cabin? Depressed about his friend?"

"What do you care?" Skinny Minnie asked. "Make like a bee and buzz off."

"Yeah, Wally, leave us alone," Buffy said.

"I just hope John's not too *crushed* about Darrell's accident," Walter said, holding back a smirk. "It was a terrible thing."

Buffy eyed her brother cautiously. "I don't know why you keep trying to be nice to us, Wally. But whatever your little plan is, it's not going to work."

Skinny Minnie nodded. "Yeah. We're not going to fall for it, so just make like a window and shut up."

Ms. Greeble set a plate of eggs and bacon on the table. "I don't know if you guys are hungry, but here it is." She scooped a big spoonful of eggs onto Minnie's plate.

"Not so much, Ms. Greeble," Minnie said. "You know I can't eat that much food."

"Picky, picky," Ms. Greeble muttered as she scooped most of the eggs off Minnie's plate and gave them to Buffy.

Walter put a mound of eggs and several strips of bacon on his plate. *I'm as hungry as a horse,* he thought. *Good thing I'm not as hungry as a raccoon, or my appetite might be a little* flat. Using his napkin, he wiped the smile from his face.

After he ate, Walter volunteered to throw away the trash.

"That's very nice of you, Walter, my boy," Mr. Smirch said. "I guess you just can't help being so generous."

"Something I learned from you, Mr. Smirch," Walter said. "Never let a day go by without performing a good deed." *Or covering up a bad one,* Walter added to himself.

"That's what I always say," Mr. Smirch agreed. "Yes, indeedy."

"You know," Walter said, unable to resist tugging Mr. Smirk's chain. "I'm going to tell Momsy how great you and your camp are. I'm sure all her friends would like a place to send their rich little children."

The counselor's smile stretched from ear to ear. "Would you? Oh, my, that would be super-duper."

"Sure," Walter said, then chortled under his breath, "Just as soon as I donate one of my kidneys to a pauper."

He chuckled evilly and picked up the bags of garbage. There was more than enough trash to bury John.

After he covered up the totem's work, Walter spent the rest of the day in his cabin.

At dinner, he could barely eat his hamburger and tater tots. Butterflies fluttered in his stomach. He looked over at his sister and her thin friend. An evil grin crept onto his face. *Who would be the next one to fall under the totem's spell?*

Would it be "See you later, Buffy Gator?" Or would Skinny Minnie turn out to be a real *boar?*

Only the morning would tell.

9
MINNIE PIGS OUT

Once again, anticipation of the morning's events had kept Walter awake most of the night. At about four o'clock, he dropped off to sleep, only to be awakened by the alarm two hours later.

He dragged himself out of bed, got dressed, then stumbled outside to hide near Minnie and Buffy's cabin. A tingle of anticipation fluttered through his belly.

"I wonder who will be starring in the creature feature today?" Walter giggled.

The door to the cabin creaked open and Buffy stepped outside. She wore a silk bathrobe and carried a towel.

"So it's Buffy the Alligator, is it?" Walter whispered.

Buffy walked out onto the damp ground and

72

yawned. It was then that Walter noticed she wasn't wearing the totem necklace.

"What? That stupid little witch," Walter hissed. "She took off the necklace!"

"You coming, Skinny Minnie?" Buffy asked as she stretched.

"Hold your horses, Buffy. I'm ready." Minnie came out of the cabin. She wore a cotton bathrobe and also carried a towel. She wasn't wearing her necklace either.

Walter shook with rage. "Those—those trolls! Why did they take them off?"

The two girls walked toward the showers. Walter watched them, his eyes burning in anger.

Fifteen minutes later, the girls returned to the cabin to get dressed.

Walter followed the girls to the covered picnic area and sat at their table. A breakfast of pancakes and sausages was already laid out before them.

"I see you're not wearing the necklaces you stole from me," Walter said. "Are you ready to give them back, now that you've had your fun?"

"Are you dreaming, Wally?" Buffy asked. "Those necklaces belong to us now."

"So where are they?"

"If you must know, mine's in my cabin," Buffy said tersely. "I took it off to take a shower, and I guess I forgot to put it back on."

"Oh, I took mine off to shower, too," Skinny Minnie said. "But mine's here in my pocket. Thanks so much for reminding me, Wally." Her words dripped with sarcasm.

"I want that back," Walter protested.

"Dream on, rich boy," Minnie said. She took the necklace from her pocket and put it around her neck.

Almost immediately, Minnie's expression changed. She wrinkled her nose and started snorting.

"What are you doing, Minnie?" Buffy giggled.

Minnie looked at her and snorted.

A devious smile crept over Walter's features. "Looks like Minnie's becoming a little *boar*ing," he said.

Minnie bent over her plate and started to devour her pancakes. She gulped them down in huge bites. Her cheeks and nose were smeared with maple syrup. When she finished eating all the pancakes on her plate, she grabbed Buffy's plate and started gobbling down the pancakes on it.

"Minnie, what's going on?" Buffy asked.

"Can't you see she's pigging out?" Walter asked, chuckling.

Minnie ate all the pancakes on Buffy's plate.

Walter shoved his plate under her nose, and she began to eat those pancakes as well.

Stack after stack of pancakes slid down the thin girl's throat. Her slurping gulps attracted the attention of the other campers. Some laughed, while others looked a little sick.

Minnie's stomach began to swell with the heavy pancakes, but she just kept eating.

Slurp. Chomp. Smack. Gulp.

"Minnie, stop it," Buffy said. "It's not funny anymore."

Skinny Minnie paid no attention. She kept stuffing her face. Filling her stomach. Fuller and fuller.

"Minnie, stop it!" Buffy cried.

Minnie grabbed a handful of sausages off the tray and gobbled them down in squishy gulps.

Walter sat back and watched as Minnie kept eating. The buttons on her shorts snapped as her belly continued to bulge.

"Mr. Smirch, something's wrong with Minnie!" Buffy cried.

Mr. Smirch stood up and patted the corners of his mouth with his napkin. He strolled over to where Minnie sat gorging herself.

"What's all the fuss?" he chirped.

"It's Skinny Minnie," Buffy cried. "She won't stop eating."

Mr. Smirch turned to Minnie. "Now, really, Minnie, making a pig of yourself is hardly fair to the other campers," he said. "I mean, we can only afford to serve so much food."

Minnie grabbed a pitcher of milk and drank it all down in one gulp. The white liquid leaked down the sides of her face.

"Stop milking it, Minnie," Walter giggled. "You won't leave room for dessert."

Buffy shot a nasty look at her brother.

And then something terrible happened. Minnie's face contorted with pain. She groaned and fell back onto the hard concrete. A trail of blood and milk leaked from the corner of her mouth.

"Minnie!" Buffy screamed.

"Oh, my goodness," Mr. Smirch said. He wrung his hands. "Her stomach must have burst. Um… Ms. Greeble, if you please? Perhaps a little antacid is in order."

"Minnie!" Buffy said. "Why did you do this?"

Minnie looked at her and squealed like a pig.

Walter laughed. "Quick, somebody put an apple in her mouth, and we'll roast her."

Buffy turned to her brother, an incredulous look on her face. "I don't know how, Walter, but you did this, didn't you? You made Minnie go crazy!"

Walter's face registered shock and hurt. "How can you say such a thing?" he asked. Then he gave Buffy an evil grin. "It's not my fault that Minnie wanted to *hog* all the breakfast!"

Buffy screamed in anger and grabbed a knife from the table. "I'm going to do something I should have done a long time ago," she said to her brother. "I'm going to carve you up and see if your heart really is made of stone!"

"Now, Buffy," Mr. Smirch said. "This is no time for a sibling spat."

"It's not a spat, Mr. Smirch. I'm going to cut out Wally by Golly's evil little heart."

"Ms. Greeble!" Mr. Smirch called. "For goodness' sake, get Buffy out of here. She's taken leave of her senses!"

"Buffy," Ms. Greeble said sternly. "Come along now. Put down the knife, and let's go back to your cabin."

"I'm not going anywhere until I see what Walter's really like inside," Buffy said, starting toward Walter.

"Um, help?" Walter squeaked, taking a shaky step backward.

Suddenly, Ms. Greeble darted forward and grabbed Buffy's wrist. She twisted the knife out of Buffy's hand, then cracked her on the knuckles with her oversize pencil.

"Come along, Buffy," Ms. Greeble said. "I have a special cabin for you."

"No! Let me go!" Buffy cried as Ms. Greeble dragged her toward the detention cabin. "Walter did this to Minnie! I have to make him pay!"

"No, you're the one who's paid," Walter said to himself. "Paid in full."

Walter felt a rising sense of triumph as he watched his sister being led away. Even if she never wore the alligator totem, he'd won.

Mr. Smirch waved his arms at the campers. "Everyone to their cabins right now!" he said.

The children kept staring at Skinny Minnie.

"Uh, snap to it, camper-wampers," Mr. Smirch said. "Minnie just needs a little time to digest her breakfast."

"Yeah, like ten years," Walter chuckled to himself.

The kids walked back to their cabins. They spoke in low whispers.

Walter tried to conceal his glee.

It wasn't until he reached the privacy of his cabin that he allowed his emotions to come out. He dove onto his bed and raised his fists in the air.

"I got them all back," Walter said. "They all paid for the way they treated me. And the great thing is, it hasn't cost me a dime."

He guffawed. "Why should I go back and pay Crooked Foot for the totems, now that they've already worked?"

Walter slapped his knee. "If he was stupid enough to give me the totems without payment, then it's his tough luck that he won't get paid."

Walter laughed until he was spent. He closed his eyes and sighed with pleasure. It had been a long couple of days. Soon he fell into a deep sleep and started dreaming.

In his dream, Walter stood in the woods and watched his victims parade by. A giant eagle carried Darrell's broken body in its talons. What was left of John rolled by in a blood-red wagon pushed by a grinning raccoon. A wild boar carried Minnie impaled on its tusks. Two alligators walked Buffy by in a white straitjacket.

Walter woke up laughing, but stopped abruptly when he heard chanting, floating ghostlike over the campground. The eerie sound traveled on a cold wind that chilled Walter's skin. He rubbed the goose bumps on his arms.

"Crooked Foot!" Walter said. "He's making a totem for me!"

A sick feeling washed over him.

"Maybe I should've paid him," Walter said. Then he shook his head. "No, I'm safe. I'd have to wear the totem for it to work."

He pulled the sheets over his ears to shut out the chanting.

But it only grew louder.

The pounding of the drum reminded him of a beating heart.

Suddenly, a cold wind blew open Walter's cabin door. Walter curled into a ball, trying to hide. His body shook with terror. Fear tugged the hair on the back of his neck.

Soft footsteps approached. It was the sound of moccasins on the wood floor.

Crooked Foot was coming to get him!

Walter wanted to throw back the sheets and cry out that he had the money. But fear locked him in place.

The steps stopped by the foot of his bunk.

"Walter?" a voice asked. "Are you okay?"

Huh?

"Walter, it's me. Mr. Smirch."

Walter peeked out from under the sheet and saw the camp director.

"Everything okely-dokely?" Mr. Smirch asked.

"Uh, yes, just fine," Walter said, throwing off the sheets. He glanced at the clock on the dresser. It was past noon.

In the window he saw Crooked Foot staring at him, his eyes hard as stone.

Walter's jaw dropped open. He tried to cry out, but could only manage a croak. He blinked, and the Indian was gone.

"I just wanted you to know that we had to take your sister to a local hospital," Mr. Smirch said. "She just needs a little time to collect herself, I'm sure."

"Huh?" Walter croaked, his mouth dry with fear.

"I said, your sister's in the hospital. She's under sedation and sleeping peacefully. They won't know anything about her condition for a few days."

"A few days," Walter mumbled.

"Yes. I tried to contact your parents, but no one was home. I left a message."

"Home?" Walter said, snapping out of his daze. The image of the Indian's cold stare burned in his mind. "Yes! I want to go home. Right now!"

Mr. Smirch smiled. "Yes, well, as I said, no one was home when I called."

"I don't care! I want to go home! And I want to go home right now!"

"Walter, we can't just take you home and leave you there by yourself. You're only eleven years old. Besides, I wanted to take you home personally, so I could meet your father and money, uh, mother. Do you happen to know where your parents might be?"

Walter glanced at the calendar on the wall and slapped his forehead. "Oh, no! They're on vacation in Paris. They won't be back until tomorrow!"

"Well, tomorrow's not that far off," Mr. Smirch said in a chipper tone. "No sirree, boy, it's just around the corner. And then we'll get you home to Mom and Pop. Maybe even get a chance to chat about our humble little camp."

Walter stamped his feet on the ground. "I have to get out of here! Today!"

Mr. Smirch put his hand on Walter's shoulder. "I know how upset you must be about your sister, but…"

"My sister?" Walter cried. "Who cares about her? I'm the one in troub—" Walter stopped himself. He was revealing too much.

Mr. Smirch wagged his finger. "Now, Walter, I know you don't mean that about your sister."

Walter took a deep breath and collected himself. "You're right," he said. "I'm just so upset, I don't know what I'm saying."

"I know. I just hope your parents are as understanding when we talk to them tomorrow about Buffy. Poor girl."

Walter nodded.

Mr. Smirch sighed and stood up. "I suppose I

should get back to the other campers. Ms. Greeble says some of them were a little upset when the ambulance took Minnie away. Anyway," he said as he left, "keep a stiff upper lip and all that."

"Right," Walter whispered. "Keep a stiff upper lip when there's a crazy Indian after my scalp."

Walter sat on his bunk and tried to come up with a plan.

"I know!" he cried. "Crooked Foot won't dare show himself in front of the other campers. I'll just go to all the stupid activities today. That way, I'll always be around other people. As for tonight..."

After a moment of thought, he smiled. "Not a problem. I'll just lock the cabin door and put tacks all over the floor. If Crooked Foot comes in wearing those deerskin moccasins of his, everybody in camp will hear it."

Walter got up to join the arts and crafts class, a confident grin on his face.

"No moth-eaten redskin can get the better of Walter Ridgemont the third," he said, strutting toward the door. "The only thing I'm going to lose tonight is a little sleep."

10
YOU GOTTA HAVE HEART

As night approached, the sun dipped toward the horizon, painting the sky a bloody red.

Walter scurried across the campgrounds toward the showers. He wanted to wash off after spending the day playing with the peasants.

At the door to the shower room, Walter paused. Something wasn't quite right. He listened, but all he could hear were the frogs and crickets singing in the slowly gathering dusk. It was the strangest feeling, almost as if…as if he were being watched!

He turned and surveyed the campgrounds. Just for a moment, he thought he glimpsed a bright patchwork shirt in the bushes.

"Just my imagination," Walter told himself. "I've got Crooked Foot on the brain."

Then he watched as the bushes swayed slightly, as if something was moving through them.

"That's just a possum or an armadillo," Walter muttered. "It's…" Walter's words caught in his throat.

It was Crooked Foot, eyes as cold as Walter's heart, glaring at him from the stand of palmettos. The Indian said nothing.

"Y-you're not scaring me, Crooked Foot," Walter managed to choke out, inching his way back toward his cabin. "I'm leaving this sorry camp tomorrow, and you can forget about your payment."

Crooked Foot remained silent.

"You're a terrible businessman," Walter cried as he took off running. "You should've made me pay you *before* you gave me the totems for my revenge. Now you'll get nothing!"

Walter ducked into the cabin and locked the door. He peered out his cabin window. Crooked Foot was gone!

"Ha!" Walter said, breathing heavily. "I'm safe now till morning."

He went to his backpack and removed the box of tacks he had stolen from the camp supplies that afternoon. He spread them in front of the door and under the window.

Satisfied with his trap, Walter climbed into bed and watched the light outside the window slowly die.

"I hope he does try to sneak in here," Walter sneered. "He can be the first member of the Tack Foot Indian tribe. Ha!"

Walter turned on his side and closed his eyes.

The night passed slowly.

At about midnight, Walter finally drifted off to sleep.

Walter started awake as a callused hand seized his shoulder.

A shadowy form stood over him. For a moment, Walter thought it was morning, and it was Mr. Smirch, coming to get him. But that couldn't be, he realized. It was still dark outside...

Walter's eyes bulged when he recognized the dark figure stooped over him—it was Crooked Foot!

"H-how did you get in here?" Walter stammered. "The tacks..."

"It's time for you to pay, Walter Ridgemont," the old Indian said, shaking him.

"Okay, okay, take it easy!" Walter said, fear shooting through him. *I've got to keep my head,* Walter thought. *This guy can't do anything to me.*

"Yeah, sure, I'll pay." He laughed. "That stuff I said before, about your being a bad businessman and all that? I was just joking with you. You know…joking?"

Crooked Foot didn't smile. "It is time for you to pay," he said again.

"Look, I was going to get the money for you tomorrow," Walter said, thinking fast. "My Momsy is sending it to me in the mail. How much do I owe you, anyway? Whatever it is, I'm sure I'll have enough."

This time, Crooked Foot smiled. "Money?" he asked. "Who said anything about money?"

Walter was confused. "Then how do I pay you back?"

"You don't pay *me* at all," the shaman said.

"Huh?"

"Whenever a person borrows the powers of the animals, he must give those animals a part of himself in return."

Walter jumped as a huge eagle shattered the window and swooped into the room. It landed on Crooked Foot's shoulder.

"You see, you borrow from the eagle, and it is the eagle that comes for payment."

A raccoon jumped through the broken window and scurried to the edge of Walter's bunk. It jumped up and rubbed its paws.

"The raccoon has come for his share as well," Crooked Foot said.

A 300-pound boar pushed open the cabin door. Its tusks gleamed in the cold moonlight.

Crooked Foot reached down and stroked the coarse bristles of the boar's head.

"I—I don't get it," Walter stammered. "W-what do these animals want from me?"

"What they are owed."

Walter swallowed hard. "And what is that?"

Crooked Foot looked at the animals.

At that moment, in the pale of the moonlight, Walter realized that he could see right through Crooked Foot! His face blanched. Crooked Foot *was* a ghost!

"In this case, rich boy," Crooked Foot said, turning back to Walter, "the pig wants your greedy eyes. The raccoon wants your grasping hands. And the eagle want your cold, cold heart."

"Nooooo!" Walter screamed as the animals rushed in to tear him apart.

EPILOGUE

The next morning, the bus arrived at Camp Pocahauntus to take the campers home. The old bus driver got out to help load the campers' suitcases. He knocked on the door of Walter's cabin.

No one answered.

The driver went in and saw Walter's mangled corpse. He rubbed his wrinkled, warty chin.

"Hmm," he said. "I always thought that Walter didn't have a heart. And now I guess I'm finally right. *Heeheeheeheehee...*"

Sure, summer camp was a scream.
But do you have the guts to visit our carnival?

A TALE FROM THE
CRYPT
CARNIVAL

"Wait a minute," Jeremy protested. "I don't want to go on this ride!"

"Too late," the barker said, strapping him in. "It's time to rot-and-roll!"

He grabbed a large lever and pulled. The Round-Up ride rumbled and started to spin.

"Let me off!" Jeremy shouted.

The ride picked up speed. Faster and faster the round cage went. The kids on the ride began to scream.

Suddenly, the floor dropped, and the kids found themselves pressed against the sides of the cage.

Jeremy closed his eyes and tried not to shriek.

Then Jeremy heard a *splat* next to his head. A few drops of something gooey stuck to his cheek. He opened his eyes and glanced over.

There was a bloody ear stuck to the cage next to him!

You *choose how the story ends,* you *suffer the consequences in Tales from the Crypt's*

It was supposed to be a party-hearty weekend in the woods. You and your friends blew off school, lied to your parents, "borrowed" a car, and headed for the abandoned campgrounds outside town.

But then things started to go wrong. Terribly wrong.

Will the moves you choose save your skin? Maybe...*Maybe not.* But don't despair. Read the book again and again until you find an ending you can live with.

But be careful not to make a blunder—or you will end up six feet under!

TALES FROM THE CRYPTKEEPER ™

See your favorite Cryptkeeper Tales come alive! Videos priced to die for! Only $12.98* each!

Chuck (and Melvin) and the Beanstalker

Dead Men Don't Jump

That's right, Crypto-kiddies! Now, you can chill out with the beastly best of my frightfully successful animated TV series...on videocassette! Each of my spine-tingling TALES FROM THE CRYPTKEEPER video volumes features TWO completely creepy episodes.

Look for these two new fiendishly fun video volumes at your favorite video out-let. Then, start your very own TALES FROM THE CRYPTKEEPER video collection. Trust me...it'll be a scream come true.

ON VIDEOCASSETTE!

SONY WONDER

TALES FROM THE CRYPTKEEPER™ & ©1994 Tales from the Crypt Holdings. All rights reserved. Manufactured by Sony Wonder, a division of Sony Music/550 Madison Avenue, New York, NY 10022-3211/"SONY WONDER" and SONY are trademarks of Sony Corporation. All rights reserved. *Suggested retail price for U.S. only.

NELVANA